BEAR IN MIND
A Book of Bear Poems
Selected by
BOBBYE S. GOLDSTEIN

ILLUSTRATED BY
WILLIAM PÈNE DU BOIS

Puffin Books

A great big bear hug for three very special people
Gabriel F. Goldstein
Lee Bennett Hopkins
Deborah Brodie
B. G.

PUFFIN BOOKS
Published by the Penguin Group
Viking Penguin, a division of Penguin Books USA Inc.,
375 Hudson Street, New York, New York 10014, U.S.A.
Penguin Books Ltd, 27 Wrights Lane, London W8 5TZ, England
Penguin Books Australia Ltd, Ringwood, Victoria, Australia
Penguin Books Canada Ltd, 2801 John Street, Markham, Ontario, Canada L3R 1B4
Penguin Books (N.Z.) Ltd, 182–190 Wairau Road, Auckland 10, New Zealand

Penguin Books Ltd, Registered Offices: Harmondsworth, Middlesex, England

First published in the United States of America by Viking Penguin Inc. 1989
Published in Picture Puffins, 1991
1   3   5   7   9   10   8   6   4   2
Copyright © Bobbye S. Goldstein, 1989
Illustrations copyright © William Pène du Bois, 1989
All rights reserved
Page 32 constitutes an extension of this copyright page.

Library of Congress Catalog Card Number: 90-50840
ISBN 0-14-050799-X

Printed in the United States of America
Set in Sabon

Contents

Springtime

BEAR COUNTRY

River-ice is melting
   and snow hangs like lace
     crusting yellow grass.

The brown bear's den is empty
   and a drowsy mother guides
     her wobbly cubs to water.

They sniff the air, feel the sun.
   Wind is stirring soft brown fur
     and wild young blood.

Lillian M. Fisher

BEAR THOUGHTS

Good-bye sleep
It's time for fun
To romp and run
In the warm spring sun.

Cecily Mopsey

WAKE-UP CALL

This morning
in all the forest
everywhere
the bears lift their heavy heads
and blink.

They wear hand-me-down
coats
left from some fat, glossy time
they have forgotten—
coats that hang dusty and loose
the pockets sagging
buttons undone.

On slow legs
still caught in the trap
of winter sleep
the bears shamble
through their open doors.

Wake up, bears!
All the news
is printed on the stones
in green velvet!

Barbara Juster Esbensen

Funny Bears, Honey Bears

THE ADVENTURES OF ISABEL

Isabel met an enormous bear,
Isabel, Isabel, didn't care.
The bear was hungry, the bear was ravenous,
The bear's big mouth was cruel and cavernous.
The bear said, Isabel, glad to meet you,
How do, Isabel, now I'll eat you!
Isabel, Isabel, didn't worry;
Isabel didn't scream or scurry.
She washed her hands and she straightened her hair up,
Then Isabel quietly ate the bear up. . . .

Ogden Nash

SAFE

A bear can GROWL
    A bear can HOWL
But not when he's
    A picture
        On my BIG
           BATH TOWEL!

Bobbye S. Goldstein

Said the bear to the dog, "You're so pale!
Oh, why do you sob so and wail?"
    Said the dog to the bear,
    "Perhaps you don't care,
But you're standing, old boy, on my tail."

Edward S. Mullins

ALGY NO MORE

Algy met a bear
The bear met Algy.
The bear grew bulgy—
The bulge was Algy.

Unknown

THE BEAR AND THE BUTTERFLY

The bear and the butterfly had a fight
All the day and most of the night
Till at last the bear lay waving his paws
And the butterfly lit on one of his jaws.
Oh, never struggle and never fight
With a butterfly on a moonlight night.

Margaret Wise Brown

Bear Facts

What's purple and shaped like a bear
With masses of long, curly hair?
　　The answer, of course,
　　Isn't cow, bird, or horse,
But a purplish, curly-haired bear.

Edward S. Mullins

ADVICE FOR HIKERS

If you find yourself in a darkish woods,
　　Beneath a darkish tree,
And you hear a growl from some place
　　Near, from something you can't see—

If you gaze between some darkish leaves
　　With your sharpest hiker's stare
And discover, looking back at you,
　　A somewhat darkish bear—

Don't stick around to analyze.
Don't stay for one more stare.
Don't pat his darkish pudgy nose.

Do this—

GET OUT OF THERE!

Isabel Joshlin Glaser

LIMERICK

A bear went in search of some honey
On a day that was golden and sunny.
When he reached in a tree,
His nose met a bee
That gave him a run for his honey.

Margaret Hillert

Wiggle waggles went the bear,
Catching bees in his underwear.
    One bee out,
    One bee in.

And one bee bit him
On his big bear skin.

Dennis Lee

MORE ABOUT BEARS

Some bears are fierce, and some are fiercer.
Few bears (I rather hope) are near, sir.
From what I know of bears, they are
Better few and better far.

John Ciardi

GRIZZLY BEAR

If you ever, ever, ever
        meet a grizzly bear,
You must never, never, never
        ask him where
He is going,
Or what he is doing;
For if you ever, ever dare
To stop a grizzly bear,
You will never
        meet another grizzly bear.

Mary Austin

Bears on View at the Circus and Zoo

A cheerful old bear at the Zoo
Could always find something to do.
    When it bored him, you know,
    To walk to and fro,
He reversed it, and walked fro and to.

Anonymous

Eight big black bears six feet tall,
each one perched on a big rubber ball,
balancing on four legs, balancing on two,
clever tricks you'd never think a bear could ever do.

Eight big black bears playing clarinets,
balancing on barrels, doing pirouettes.
Standing on their heads and hopping over chairs,
eight very talented big black bears.

Jack Prelutsky

THE BEAR

A bear got loose from the city Zoo,
He came up the street and said,
      "How do you do?"
I shook his paw and said with a smile,
"I'm fine—please stay and play awhile."

Said the big fuzzy bear,
Without ruffling a hair,
      "I'd like some bread,
      And I'd like some honey;
      But the trouble is,
      I have no money."

So I bought a honey sandwich fat,
And he gobbled it down just like that.
Then he turned so quickly and said, "good-bye,
Back to the Zoo I must surely fly.
      I want to go home, I do,
      I'm homesick for the Zoo."

I looked around—
      there was nothing there;
Up in thin air
      had vanished that bear!

Lois Lenski

POLAR BEAR

The Polar Bear never makes his bed;
He sleeps on a cake of ice instead.
He has no blanket, no quilt, no sheet
Except the rain and snow and sleet.
He drifts about on a white ice floe
While cold winds howl and blizzards blow
And the temperature drops to forty below.
The Polar Bear never makes his bed;
The blanket he pulls up over his head
Is lined with soft and feathery snow.
If ever he rose and turned on the light,
He would find a world of bathtub white,
And icebergs floating through the night.

William Jay Smith

THE POLAR BEAR

The polar bear by being white
gives up his camouflage at night.
And yet, without a thought or care,
he wanders here, meanders there,
and gaily treads the icy floes
completely unconcerned with foes.
For after dark nobody dares
to set out after polar bears.

Jack Prelutsky

BEARS

I wouldn't be a bear
for several reasons.

My main objection
has to do with seasons:

For one thing, I'd not like
hot fur in summer,

But then, I think the winters
would be dumber—

Imagine! curling up where
there's no heating

And sleeping months and months
and never eating . . .
        NEVER EATING!

Aileen Fisher

BEAR COAT

The polar bear, the
  Polar bear—
He has a handsome
  Coat to wear.

But, while it's thick and
  Warm and white,
He has to wear it day and
  Night.

And when the summer
  Comes, poor brute,
He wears it for his swimming
  Suit.

Although his coat is thought
  So fine,
I'm very glad that it's
  Not mine.

Leland B. Jacobs

POLAR BEAR

The secret of the polar bear
Is that he wears long underwear.

Gail Kredenser

Sleep Time

BEAR CUB'S DAY

Black bear cub trotted after his mother,
Tumbled and tussled in play with his brother,
Romped and roared in a wrestling match,
Snatched some lunch in a blueberry patch,
Climbed tall trees without any fear,
Fished for fish where the stream ran clear,
Curled at last in a furry heap,
Too tired for anything else but sleep.

Margaret Hillert

GRANDPA BEAR'S LULLABY

The night is long
But fur is deep.
You will be warm
In winter sleep.

The food is gone
But dreams are sweet
And they will be
Your winter meat.

The cave is dark
But dreams are bright
And they will serve
As winter light.

Sleep, my little cubs, sleep.

Jane Yolen

BIG HAIRY FISHERMAN

Big hairy fisherman, shaggy brown bear,
Spring has coaxed you from your lair.
The day is warm, you drowse in sun
Dreaming of salmon soon to run.

Lazy old fisherman asleep on the shore,
Seagulls are screaming, a dozen or more.
Hungry and greedy, they loudly entreat,
"Time to go fishing, get up on your feet!"

Sleepytime fisherman, giant brown beast,
The stream bed is ripe for your salmon feast.
But leave a few tidbits when you are through.
The seagulls are waiting and they're hungry, too!

Lillian M. Fisher

A bear cub, too tired to play,
Decided to call it a day.
  So he fastened the lock,
  Then wound up his clock
And set it for quarter-past May.

Edmund S. Mullins

Bears sleep,
Bears snooze,
To while away
Cold winter blues!

Cecily Mopsey

THE BLACK BEAR

In the summer, fall and spring
the black bear sports and has his fling,

but winter sends him straight indoors
and there he snores . . . and snores . . . and snores.

Jack Prelutsky

24

Teddy Bear Time

TEDDY BEAR

Teddy Bear, Teddy Bear, turn around
Teddy Bear, Teddy Bear, touch the ground.
Teddy Bear, Teddy Bear, show your shoe
Teddy Bear, Teddy Bear, that will do.

Teddy Bear, Teddy Bear, go up stairs
Teddy Bear, Teddy Bear, say your prayers.
Teddy Bear, Teddy Bear, turn out the light
Teddy Bear, Teddy Bear, say good night.

NIGHT BEAR

In the dark of night
    when all is still
And I'm half-sleeping in my bed;

It's good to know
    my Teddy-bear
is snuggling at my head.

Lee Bennett Hopkins

MY TEDDY BEAR

A teddy bear is a faithful friend.
You can pick him up at either end.
His fur is the color of breakfast toast,
And he's always there when you need him most.

Marchette Chute

IT'S NOT VERY FAIR

It's not very fair
For a bear in a lair
Not to come out
Except on a dare.

So I'll settle for Teddy
Who's willing and ready
For a romp on the rug
And a cuddle and hug.

Bobbye S. Goldstein

THE BEAR WITH GOLDEN HAIR

Long ago
There was a bear
With ice-blue eyes
And golden hair
And pale-pink paws,
A bright black nose,
And a shiny, silken ribbon
More red than rose.

But though he was a perfect bear,
He had one secret, deep despair:
He did not have a thing to wear
Except a lot of golden hair.
"I wish,"
He'd sigh,
"I had a pair
Of socks or shoes
In reds or blues.
Some pale-plaid pants
I'd also choose."
For hours he would sit and muse
On splendid clothes
That he would wear
Were he not such a fair-haired bear.

One Wednesday
Also long ago,
This gold-haired bear
Went to and fro
To see the spring
And sniff the bud,
When Amelia Ellen Whitely,
Who was holding him quite tightly,
Tripped a little more than slightly
And he fell into the mud.

Amelia Ellen had to stare.
There lay her once-so-golden bear
Now muddied up from here to there.

Now muddied down from there to here,
From toe to toe
To ear to ear
To heel to heel
To knee to nose;
His ribbon hanging limply down,
A wet and brackish
Blackish brown,
A lot more mud than rose.

She took him home
And ran the tub
And started in to soap and scrub,
To comb and brush,
To rinse and rub.
From dusk she worked
Into the dawn,
And as the sunlight lit the lawn
No mud was there upon her bear.
But, oh,
Amelia had to stare,
His hair was also gone.

Then, her needle threaded tightly,
Amelia Ellen Whitely
Stitched with energy and care
Daily, noon, and nightly.
She made bear pairs
Of socks and shoes
In rosey reds and azure blues,
Jackets,
Gloves,
And pale-plaid pants
At which each passerby would glance,
Exclaiming with approving "ohs."
"I say, my dear,
Do give a stare
At yonder very-well-dressed bear.
If I but had such splendid clothes."

Long ago
There was a bear
Without a single golden hair.
He also did not have a care.
Oh, happy hair-free carefree bear.

Karla Kuskin

Grateful acknowledgment is made to the following for permission to reprint copyrighted material:

Marchette Chute for "My Teddy Bear" from *Rhymes About Us*. Copyright 1974 by Marchette Chute. Reprinted by permission of the author.

Blackie and Son Ltd. and Stan Colbert of the Colbert Agency Inc. for "Wiggle Waggles Went the Bear" from *Jelly Belly* by Dennis Lee. © 1983 Dennis Lee.

Lois Lenski Covey Foundation for "The Bear" from *City Poems* by Lois Lenski.

Curtis Brown Ltd. for "Night Bear" from *Surprises* by Lee Bennett Hopkins. Copyright © 1972 by Lee Bennett Hopkins. "Grandpa Bear" from *Dragon Night and Other Lullabies* by Jane Yolen. Copyright © 1981 by Jane Yolen. Reprinted by permission of Curtis Brown Ltd.

Aileen Fisher for "Bears" from *Up the Windy Hill*, Abelard, New York, 1953. Copyright renewed 1981 by Aileen Fisher. By permission of the author.

Lillian M. Fisher for "Big Hairy Fisherman" and "Bear Country." Copyright © 1987 by Lillian M. Fisher. By permission of the author who controls all rights.

Isabel Joshlin Glaser for "Advice for Hikers." Used by permission of the author, who controls all rights.

Greenwillow Books for "The Polar Bear," Copyright © 1970, 1983 by Jack Prelutsky, and "The Black Bear," Copyright © 1974, 1983 by Jack Prelutsky, from *Zoo Doings* by Jack Prelutsky. By permission of Greenwillow Books, a division of William Morrow and Company, Inc.

Harper & Row, Publishers, Inc. for "The Bear and the Butterfly" from *Nibble Nibble* by Margaret Wise Brown (Young Scott Books). Text copyright © 1959 by William R. Scott, Inc. "More About Bears" from *You Read to Me, I'll Read to You* by John Ciardi. Copyright © 1962 by John Ciardi. "Wake-Up Call" from *Cold Stars and Fireflies* by Barbara Juster Esbensen. Copyright © 1984 by Barbara Juster Esbensen. "The Bear with Golden Hair" from *Dogs and Dragons, Trees and Dreams* by Karla Kuskin. Copyright © 1964 by Karla Kuskin. Reprinted by permission of Harper & Row, Publishers, Inc.

Margaret Hillert for "Bear Cub's Day" and "Limerick." Used by permission of the author, who controls all rights.

Henry Holt and Company, Inc. for "Bear Coat" from *Just Around the Corner* by Leland B. Jacobs. Copyright © 1964 by Leland B. Jacobs. Reprinted by permission of Henry Holt and Company, Inc.

Houghton Mifflin Company for "Grizzly Bear" from *The Children Sing in the Far West* by Mary Austin. Copyright 1928 by Mary Austin. Copyright © renewed 1956 by Kenneth M. Chapman and Mary C. Wheelwright. Reprinted by permission of Houghton Mifflin Company.

Little, Brown and Company and Curtis Brown Ltd. for the first stanza from "Adventures of Isabel" from *Custard and Company* by Odgen Nash. Copyright 1936 by Ogden Nash. By permission of Little, Brown and Company and Curtis Brown Ltd.

Gail Kredenser Mack for "Polar Bear."

Macmillan Publishing Company for "Eight Big Black Bears" from *Circus!* by Jack Prelutsky. Copyright © 1974 by Jack Prelutsky. Reprinted with permission of Macmillan Publishing Company.

Cecily Mopsey for "Bear Thoughts" and "Bears Sleep."

Platt & Munk, Publishers for selections from *The Big Book of Limericks* by Edward S. Mullins. Copyright © 1969 by Edward S. Mullins. Reprinted by permission of Platt & Munk, Publishers.

William Jay Smith for "Polar Bear" from *Laughing Time: Nonsense Poems*, published by Delacorte Press, 1980. Copyright © 1955, 1957, 1980 by William Jay Smith. Reprinted by permission of William Jay Smith.

The United Educators, Inc. for "Teddy Bear, Teddy Bear."

NASCAR RACING

Jeff Gordon

by Kristal Leebrick

Consultant:
Betty L. Carlan
Research Librarian
International Motorsports Hall of Fame
Talladega, Alabama

Capstone
press

Mankato, Minnesota

Edge Books are published by Capstone Press,
151 Good Counsel Drive, P.O. Box 669, Mankato, Minnesota 56002.
www.capstonepress.com

Library of Congress Cataloging-in-Publication Data
Leebrick, Kristal, 1958–
    Jeff Gordon / by Kristal Leebrick.
    p. cm.—(Edge Books. NASCAR racing)
    Summary: Explores the life and racing career of NASCAR Winston Cup
champion Jeff Gordon.
    ISBN-13: 978-0-7368-2424-8 (hardcover)
    ISBN-10: 0-7368-2424-3 (hardcover)
    ISBN-13: 978-0-7368-5230-2 (softcover pbk.)
    ISBN-10: 0-7368-5230-1 (softcover pbk.)
    1. Gordon, Jeff, 1971– —Juvenile literature. 2. Automobile racing drivers—
United States—Biography—Juvenile literature. [1. Gordon, Jeff, 1971– 2. Automobile
racing drivers.] I. Title.
GV1032.G67L44 2004
796.72'092—dc22   2003014782

Editorial Credits
Matt Doeden, editor; Jason Knudson, designer; Jo Miller, photo researcher

Photo Credits
Artemis Images/Indianapolis Motor Speedway, 5, 6
Getty Images/Robert Laberge, 23; Rusty Jarrett, 27; Steve Swope, 17;
    Vincent Laforet, 21
SportsChrome-USA, cover (portrait), 20; Brian Spurlock, cover (car), 28;
    Greg Crisp, 15
Sports Gallery, Inc., 8, 11, 24
The Sporting News/Bob Leverone, 19

2 3 4 5 6 09 08 07 06 05

Table of Contents

CHAPTER 1

A Young Star

On August 6, 1994, more than 250,000 fans stood and cheered at the Indianapolis Motor Speedway. NASCAR's newest star, Jeff Gordon, was battling for the lead in the first Brickyard 400. Jeff had once lived in nearby Pittsboro, Indiana. For years, he had dreamed of racing at Indy.

Late in the race, Jeff's colorful Chevrolet trailed only Ernie Irvan's Ford. Jeff pulled his car alongside Irvan and passed him on the outside. Irvan swerved low to regain the lead. The drivers stomped on the gas pedals as they sped down the track's long straightaways. They eased into their brakes as they entered the turns.

Jeff (#24) took the lead late in the 1994 Brickyard 400.

Learn about:

➜ Jeff's Brickyard 400 win

➜ Jeff as a child

➜ Jeff's early racing career

Jeff celebrated in the winner's circle after his Brickyard 400 win.

The two drivers traded the lead several times as they raced around the track. Neither driver could pull far ahead. The race looked like it would have a tight finish.

With five laps to go, Irvan began to slow down. Jeff could tell Irvan was having trouble handling his car. Suddenly, one of Irvan's tires exploded. Jeff took the lead and held off Brett Bodine to earn one of the most important wins of his career. He was only 23 years old.

Jeff's win in the Brickyard 400 was only the second win of his NASCAR career. But it helped start a streak of successes that has made him one of the most famous NASCAR drivers ever.

". . . I don't know if any win will ever top that first Brickyard 400. I'd have to say that was the all-time win for me."
—Jeff Gordon, www.jeffgordon.com, 2001

About Jeff Gordon

Today, Jeff remains one of the top stock car drivers in the world. He drives the number 24 Chevrolet. Jeff has won four NASCAR titles and more than 60 races.

Jeff was born August 4, 1971, in Vallejo, California. He grew up with his mother, Carol, older sister, Kim, and stepfather, John Bickford.

Jeff drives the number 24 DuPont Chevrolet.

Jeff became interested in racing at a young age. He was only 1 when John took him to his first race. Jeff began racing BMX bikes when he was 4.

John gave Jeff and his sister a quarter midget race car when Jeff was 5. These small cars look like go-karts. Jeff practiced driving it in parking lots near his home. He soon entered organized races. At age 8, he won his first quarter midget national championship.

Jeff's family thought he had the talent to be a professional driver. When Jeff was 13, the family moved to Florida so he could race sprint cars. When Jeff was in high school, the family moved to Indiana. Tracks in Indiana allowed drivers Jeff's age to compete against older drivers.

Jeff continued to race throughout high school. He graduated from Tri-West High School in Lizton, Indiana, in 1989. The night of his graduation, he was in a dirt track race in Bloomington, Indiana.

CHAPTER 2

Joining NASCAR

Jeff continued his racing success after high school. At age 19, he won the 1990 U.S. Auto Club national midget championship. When he was 20, he won the Silver Crown title for sprint cars.

Early in his career, Jeff traveled with his stepfather to races across the Midwest. The family lived off the money Jeff earned from these races. Jeff and John often slept in their pickup because they did not have enough money for a motel room.

Jeff always dreamed of becoming a professional driver.

Learn about:

→ The Buck Baker Driving School

→ Jeff's Busch Series career

→ Jeff's Winston Cup start

11

Stock Car Driver

Racing experts noticed Jeff's talent. In 1990, the ESPN TV network made a deal with John. ESPN paid for Jeff to attend the famous Buck Baker Driving School in Rockingham, North Carolina. In exchange, ESPN filmed Jeff's experience to show on TV.

Jeff drove a stock car for the first time at the school. He proved that he was a skilled stock car driver. Jeff believed his talents were perfect for stock car racing.

A year later, Jeff agreed to drive a Pontiac in NASCAR's Busch Grand National Series. Jeff called John and told him to sell all his old racing equipment. Jeff was going to be a professional stock car driver.

"The first time I got into a stock car, I loved it to death. It felt right."
—Jeff Gordon, www.gordonline.com

Career Statistics

Jeff Gordon

Year	Starts	Wins	Top-5s	Top-10s	Winnings
1992	1	0	0	0	$6,285
1993	30	0	7	11	$765,168
1994	31	2	7	14	$1,779,523
1995	31	7	17	23	$4,347,343
1996	31	10	21	24	$3,428,485
1997	32	10	22	23	$6,375,658
1998	33	13	26	28	$9,306,584
1999	34	7	18	21	$5,121,361
2000	34	3	11	22	$2,703,586
2001	36	6	18	24	$10,879,757
2002	36	3	13	20	$7,189,305
2003	36	3	14	20	$5,107,760
Career	365	64	174	230	$57,101,815

Early Success

Jeff quickly proved that he was a talented NASCAR driver. In 1991, he earned 11 Busch poles by running the fastest qualifying lap. He also won three races. He was named the Busch Series Rookie of the Year.

Winston Cup car owner Rick Hendrick saw Jeff's success. He asked Jeff to join his racing team. Jeff made his first Winston Cup start in the last race of the 1992 season. He was 21 years old.

In 1993, Jeff joined the Winston Cup Series full time. He drove the number 24 DuPont Chevrolet. The Daytona 500 was his first race. He won the 125-mile (200-kilometer) qualifying race before the main event. He then finished fifth in the Daytona 500.

Jeff did not win any races in 1993. But he finished second twice and had seven top-5 finishes. His colorful car and the pit crew's uniforms earned his team the nickname "Rainbow Warriors." After the season, Jeff was named Winston Cup's Rookie of the Year.

Jeff drove the Baby Ruth car in the Busch Series.

CHAPTER 3

Becoming a Legend

Jeff won two races in 1994. His first win was at the Coca-Cola 600 in Charlotte, North Carolina. After the race, Jeff cried in the winner's circle because he was so happy. Later that year, he won the first Brickyard 400. He was quickly becoming one of the biggest stars in NASCAR.

Jeff earned his first two NASCAR wins in 1994.

Learn about:

→ Jeff's first win
→ A Winston Cup title
→ A record-setting season

NASCAR Champion

Jeff entered the 1995 season hoping to finish among the top five Winston Cup drivers. Few experts believed the young driver could beat NASCAR stars such as Dale Earnhardt and Rusty Wallace. But Jeff proved that he could. He amazed fans by winning seven races in 1995.

Jeff enjoyed his early success. But some fans and drivers disliked him because of it. Earnhardt became one of Jeff's biggest rivals. Earnhardt gave Jeff the nickname "Wonder Boy." Jeff's crew chief, Ray Evernham, thought the nickname was an insult. He asked Earnhardt not to use it anymore. Instead, Earnhardt used it even more often.

Jeff and Earnhardt also battled on the track. In the 1995 season's final race, Jeff clinched the Winston Cup title. He beat Earnhardt by 34 points to become NASCAR's youngest Winston Cup champion. He was 24.

Dale Earnhardt was one of Jeff's biggest rivals on the track.

Jeff crossed the finish line inches ahead of Terry Labonte to win the 1997 Daytona 500.

More Success

Jeff had another great year in 1996. He won 10 races. But he also had some bad finishes. He failed to complete several races. These bad finishes cost him a championship. He lost the Winston Cup title to Terry Labonte by 37 points.

Jeff came back even stronger in 1997. He won the first two races of the year. Later, he had one of his most exciting victories at Bristol Motor Speedway.

With only a few laps left, Jeff was second behind Rusty Wallace. On the final turn, Jeff bumped into Wallace's back bumper. Wallace's car drifted to the outside of the track. Jeff drove low on the track to take the win. Jeff finished the season with 10 wins and his second Winston Cup title.

Jeff had a record-setting year in 1998. He tied a NASCAR record with 13 wins. He also tied a record by winning four races in a row. At one point, he had nine top-5 finishes in a row. Seven of those finishes were wins. No NASCAR driver had ever had such a dominant stretch of racing. He won the Winston Cup title by 364 points.

Jeff dominated the 1998 NASCAR season with 13 wins.

CHAPTER 4

Recent Success

Jeff struggled during the 1999 and 2000 seasons. He won seven races in 1999, but bad finishes kept him from winning another title. His crew chief, Ray Evernham, also left the team during the 1999 season.

In 2000, Jeff won only three races. He finished ninth in the standings. Some experts said Jeff would never be as good without Evernham on his team.

Jeff won seven races in 1999.

Learn about:

→ Struggles on the track
→ A fourth championship
→ Car ownership

Jeff won his fourth NASCAR title in 2001.

A Comeback

The 2001 season began badly for NASCAR. A crash in the Daytona 500 killed Dale Earnhardt. Earnhardt's death was hard on Jeff. The next week, Jeff wore a Dale Earnhardt hat during interviews. He said Earnhardt had taught him how to be a winning NASCAR driver.

Jeff won six races in 2001 and beat Tony Stewart for the Winston Cup title. He became only the third driver to win four championships.

Jeff began the 2002 season slowly. He did not win any races during the first half of the season. But he improved late in the season and won three races. One of the wins was at Bristol, where he again bumped Wallace on the last lap to take the lead. Jeff finished fourth in the standings.

The Future

Today, Jeff is not just a NASCAR driver. He is also a car owner. Jeff and Rick Hendrick own the number 48 Chevrolet. Jimmie Johnson drives the car. Many racing experts say that Johnson reminds them of Jeff. With Jeff's help, Johnson has become a top Winston Cup driver. He finished fifth in the 2002 standings, only seven points behind Jeff.

Jeff says that he does not know how long he will continue racing. He is still a young driver in a sport where stars can have success late into their 40s. He has a lifetime contract with Hendrick Motorsports. Jeff says that he plans to continue racing as long as it remains fun.

"I am trying to find time to enjoy what I've achieved. I realize that my worst day is no comparison to what some people have to deal with in their lives."
—Jeff Gordon, *The Charlotte Observer*, 5-24-03

Jeff is part owner of the car driven by Jimmie Johnson.

2001
NASCAR WINSTON CUP CHAMPION
JEFF GORDON
NASCAR Winston Cup Series
2001
DUPONT
AUTOMOTIVE
FINISHES
GOODYEAR

Career Highlights

1990   Jeff wins the 1990 U.S. Auto Club national midget championship.

1991   Jeff wins Rookie of the Year Award for the Busch Grand National Series.

1992   Jeff makes his first start in the Winston Cup Series.

1993   Jeff is named Rookie of the Year in the Winston Cup Series and becomes the first driver to win rookie honors in NASCAR's top two divisions.

1994   Jeff wins his first two Winston Cup Series races.

1995   At 24, Jeff becomes the youngest driver to win the Winston Cup championship.

1997   Jeff wins 10 races and his second championship.

1998   Jeff wins a record 13 races, including four in a row, and his third Winston Cup title.

1999   Jeff becomes the youngest driver to win the Daytona 500 twice.

2000   Jeff becomes the youngest driver in Winston Cup history to win 50 races in his career.

2001   Jeff becomes only the third driver to win four Winston Cup championships.

2003   Jeff starts his 350th consecutive Winston Cup race.

Glossary

crew chief (KROO CHEEF)—the member of a racing team who is in charge of the car and the crew; the crew chief also helps the driver choose racing strategies.

pole (POHL)—the spot at the front of the line at the beginning of a race

quarter midget (KWOR-tur MIJ-it)—a small racing vehicle that looks like a go-kart

rookie (RUK-ee)—a first-year driver

series (SIHR-eez)—a group of races that makes up one season; drivers earn points for finishing races in a series.

straightaway (STRAYT-uh-way)—a long, straight part of a racetrack

Read More

Bisson, Terry. *Tradin' Paint: Raceway Rookies and Royalty.* New York: Scholastic, 2001.

Gigliotti, Jim. *Jeff Gordon: Simply the Best.* The World of NASCAR. Excelsior, Minn.: Tradition Books, 2003.

Johnstone, Michael. *NASCAR.* The Need for Speed. Minneapolis: LernerSports, 2002.

Useful Addresses

Hendrick Motorsports
4400 Papa Joe Hendrick Boulevard
Charlotte, NC 28262

The Jeff Gordon Fan Club
Autograph Request/Fan Mail
P.O. Box 910
Harrisburg, NC 28075

NASCAR
P.O. Box 2875
Daytona Beach, FL 32120

Internet Sites

FactHound offers a safe, fun way to find Internet sites related to this book. All of the sites on FactHound have been researched by our staff.

Here's how:

1. Visit *www.facthound.com*
2. Type in this special code **0736824243** for age-appropriate sites. Or enter a search word related to this book for a more general search.
3. Click on the **Fetch It** button.

FactHound will fetch the best sites for you!

Index